The house smells like a fancy bakery. Hazel loves to bake with her dad. Most of all, she loves to try the desserts they make right after they come out of the oven, even if it's breakfast time! Dad says it's okay to have dessert for breakfast if you don't do it every day.

CYNTHIA CLIFF

PIE for BREAKFAST

A BAKING BOOK FOR CHILDREN

PRESTEL

Munich · London · New York

As Hazel eats she has an idea: "I could organize a bake sale for the school's fair!" Last year the money raised during the fair was used to buy new playground equipment. This year the money will go to the school library. Hazel loves the library as much as she loves baking.

"I'll ask all my friends for help.
We'll need lots of desserts to sell.
It will be just like a fancy bakery,
but run by kids!" says Hazel.

Hazel and her friend Amelia bought
berries at the farmers' market.
They are making two cakes,
one for the bake sale and one
for themselves!

BLACKBERRY CRUMB CAKE

1.
Preheat the oven to 350 degrees Fahrenheit/180 degrees Celsius. Grease and flour the bottom and sides of a 10 inch/26 cm springform pan. Melt ¼ cup/60g butter on a low setting in the microwave or on your stove (if you have a grown-up to help you), and let it cool.

2.
To make the cake, first sift together the flour, sugar, baking powder, and salt. Then add the milk, cooled melted butter, egg, and vanilla to the flour mixture and mix well.

3.
Pour the batter into the prepared pan. Layer the berries evenly over the batter.

4.
To make the topping, melt the butter, then combine with the sugar, cinnamon, and flour. Sprinkle this crumble topping evenly over the berries. Bake for 45–55 minutes until a knife inserted into the center comes out clean.

Makes one 10 inch/26 cm cake

CAKE INGREDIENTS

1½ cups/210g **flour**
¾ cup/150g **sugar**
2 teaspoons **baking powder**
¼ teaspoon **salt**
⅔ cup/160ml **milk**
¼ cup/60g **butter**
1 large **egg**
1 teaspoon **vanilla**
2 cups/300g **blackberries**

TOPPING INGREDIENTS

¼ cup/60g **butter**
½ cup/100g **sugar**
½ teaspoon **cinnamon**
⅓ cup/45g **flour**

Tim and his little brother Theo
decide to make muffins together.
Theo is not very helpful at first.

PEAR-GINGER MUFFINS

Makes 18 standard-sized muffins
or approximately 28 mini muffins

INGREDIENTS

2½ cups/350g **flour**
1½ teaspoons **baking powder**
1 teaspoon **powdered ginger**
pinch of **salt**
⅞ cup/200g **butter**
¾ cup/150g **brown sugar**
6 tablespoons **sugar**
¼ cup/60ml **milk**
2 **large eggs**
1 teaspoon **vanilla extract**
1 tablespoon **ginger root,
peeled and grated**
2 **ripe pears**
(the best varieties to use are
Bartlett, D'Anjou or Bosc)

1.

Preheat the oven to 325 degrees Fahrenheit/
160 degrees Celsius. Mix together the dry
ingredients—the flour, baking powder, powered
ginger, and salt. Set aside.

2.

In this step, you can use a stand mixer with a
grown-up's help. In a large bowl, cream together
the butter and sugars until light and fluffy.
Add the milk, eggs, and vanilla. Stir until blended
and then add the dry ingredients and mix well.
The batter will be very stiff.

3.

Because you have to use a knife or a vegetable
peeler, and grate the peeled ginger, ask a grown-
up for help. Carefully peel the ginger root and
grate finely. Peel, core, and dice the pears. Add the
ginger and pears to the batter and mix together.

4.

Line the muffin tin wells with paper liners.
Spoon the batter into the liners until three-
quarters full. Bake the standard-sized muffins
for 30–35 minutes, and the mini muffins for
20–25 minutes. The muffin tops will not be
very dark in color.

Camilla is making empanadas for the
bake sale, just like her abuela makes.
She will fill them with the pumpkin
that they canned from their garden.

PUMPKIN EMPANADAS

The amount of pastry you use will determine how many empanadas you can make. The filling is enough for approximately 16 pies if they are 4 inches/10 cm in diameter.

Pre-made pastry dough, or you can make your own

FILLING INGREDIENTS

1 cup/225g pumpkin puree (not pumpkin pie filling)
¼ cup/50g brown sugar
1 teaspoon heavy cream
1 teaspoon cinnamon
¼ teaspoon ground allspice

TOPPING INGREDIENTS

1 egg
1 tablespoon water
1 tablespoon sugar
1 teaspoon cinnamon

1.
Pre-heat the oven to 400 degrees Fahrenheit/200 degrees Celsius. Stir together all the ingredients for the filling in a medium bowl, then set aside.

2.
Place the unbaked pastry dough on a lightly floured surface. Using a large, round cookie cutter or a bowl that is around 4 inches/10 cm wide, cut some circles out of the dough. The amount of dough you are using will determine how many circles you will get.

3.
Take your round cutouts and place 1 tablespoon of the pumpkin filling in the center of each one. Moisten the outside edges with some water. Fold the dough in half into a half-moon shape. Seal the edges using a fork and cut a slit in the top of each pie for the steam to escape.

4.
Place your filled empanadas on a greased cookie sheet so they do not touch each other. Beat the egg with the water. Mix the sugar and cinnamon together. Brush the top of each empanada with the egg mixture, and sprinkle the sugar and cinnamon mixture on top. Bake for 20 minutes, until golden-brown.

Anna wants to make zucchini cookies. Her father is not sure he will like them, even though she is using his favorite chocolate chips.

ZUCCHINI OATMEAL COOKIES
with CHOCOLATE CHIPS

Makes approximately 20 cookies

INGREDIENTS

⅓ cup/80ml **vegetable oil**

1 large **egg**

1 teaspoon **vanilla**

⅓ cup/70g **brown sugar**

1½ cups/120g **quick oats**

1 cup/140g **flour**

½ teaspoon **baking powder**

¼ teaspoon **baking soda**

½ teaspoon **cinnamon**

¼ teaspoon **nutmeg**

½ teaspoon **salt**

½ cup/85g **chocolate chips (any flavor)**

½ cup/65g **chopped walnuts (optional)**

1 cup/230g **finely grated zucchini**

1.
Preheat the oven to 350 degrees Fahrenheit/ 180 degrees Celsius. In a large bowl, mix together the oil, egg, and vanilla, then stir in the brown sugar and mix well.

2.
In a separate bowl, stir together the dry ingredients—the oats, flour, baking powder, baking soda, spices, and salt—until well blended.

3.
Add the dry ingredients to the egg and sugar mixture, and stir until everything is combined. Then mix in the chocolate chips and the nuts, if you are using them. Gently stir the grated zucchini into the batter. The batter will be stiff.

4.
Form into 1½ inch/4 cm balls and place them onto a greased or a parchment-lined baking sheet so that they do not touch each other. Bake the cookies for 13–14 minutes, or until they are golden-brown.

Everyone in Daniel's family loves chocolate, even his baby sister, so Daniel wants to make a chocolate cake for the fair.

VEGAN CHOCOLATE CAKE

1.

Preheat the oven to 350 degrees Fahrenheit/ 180 degrees Celsius, and grease and flour two 9 inch/ 23 cm round cake pans. In a small bowl, mix together the almond milk and vinegar, and set aside so that the milk will curdle slightly.

2.

In a large bowl, put the flour, sugar, cocoa powder, baking powder, baking soda, and salt. Whisk to combine.

3.

In a separate bowl, mix together the oil, applesauce, vanilla, and almond milk and vinegar mixture. Add these wet ingredients to the flour mixture and stir until combined.

4.

With a grown-up's help, carefully pour the boiling water into the cake batter, continuing to mix until the water is worked into the batter. The batter will be very runny, which is the way it should be. Divide the batter evenly between your cake pans and bake for 30–35 minutes, or until a toothpick inserted into the center comes out clean.

5.

To make the frosting, combine the ingredients and mix well until smooth and creamy. After the cakes are completely cool, remove them from the pans. You can add frosting between the layers and to the top of the cake, and even to the sides as well. If you like, you can decorate the cake with fresh fruit, edible flowers, or sprinkles.

Makes one 9 inch/23 cm round, two-layer cake

CAKE INGREDIENTS

1 cup/240ml **unsweetened almond milk**
1 tablespoon **apple cider vinegar**
2 cups/280g **flour**
1¾ cups/350g **sugar**
¾ cup/75g **cocoa powder**
2 teaspoons **baking powder**
1½ teaspoons **baking soda**
1 teaspoon **salt**
½ cup/120ml **melted coconut oil**
(or canola oil)
⅔ cup/160ml **unsweetened applesauce**
1 tablespoon **vanilla extract**
1 cup/240ml **boiling water**

CHOCOLATE BUTTERCREAM FROSTING

1 cup/115g **cocoa powder**
1½ cups/325g **vegan butter, softened**
4 cups/450g **powdered sugar**
2 teaspoons **pure vanilla extract**
¼ cup/60ml **unsweetened almond milk**
1 cup/240ml **boiling water**

Samuel is going to make his favorite banana cake. His sister Esther is going to help him caramelize the sugar.

CARAMELIZED UPSIDE-DOWN BANANA CAKE

1.

Preheat the oven to 350 degrees Fahrenheit/ 180 degrees Celsius and grease your rectangular pan. To make the upside-down part, in a small saucepan over medium heat, melt the butter and stir in the brown sugar. Be sure to ask a grown-up for help when using the stove. Stir this mixture while cooking for 2 minutes, and then pour it evenly into the greased pan.

2.

Slice the 5 bananas in half lengthwise, then arrange on top of the sugar mixture in the bottom of the pan. Set aside.

3.

To make the cake, in a large bowl, mix together the 2 mashed bananas, melted butter, eggs, yogurt, sugar, and vanilla until all ingredients are combined to make a batter.

4.

In another bowl, stir together the flour, baking powder and salt. Add this flour mixture to the batter and stir until combined. Spread the batter evenly on top of the bananas and sugar in the baking pan. Bake for 30 minutes, until the top is golden-brown. It is important to let the cake cool so that the caramelized sugar sets, before you turn the cake out upside-down over a serving tray.

Makes one 9x13 inch/23x33 cm rectangular cake

UPSIDE-DOWN PART INGREDIENTS

7 tablespoons/100g **butter**
½ cup/100g **brown sugar**
5 **bananas**

CAKE INGREDIENTS

2 **mashed bananas**
6 tablespoons/85g **butter, melted**
2 **large eggs**
⅔ cup/160ml **Greek yogurt**
1 cup/200g **sugar**
2 teaspoons **vanilla**
2 cups/280g **flour**
4 teaspoons **baking powder**
1 teaspoon **salt**

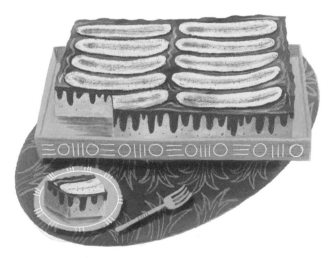

Erin enjoys making her desserts beautiful. She is decorating her tarts with fresh fruit and edible flowers.

EASY JAM TARTS

The number of tarts you can make will depend on the size of your tart molds and the amount of pastry dough you have.

PASTRY INGREDIENTS
(OR USE A STORE-BOUGHT PASTRY DOUGH)

1⅔ cups/230g **flour**
½ cup/110g **butter, cubed**
pinch of **salt**
2 to 3 tablespoons **water (cold)**

FILLING INGREDIENTS

Your favorite pre-made fruit jam or lemon curd

DECORATING INGREDIENTS

Fresh fruit, whipped cream, or edible flowers like pansies or violets

1.

Preheat the oven to 350 degrees Fahrenheit/180 degrees Celsius and lightly grease your tart molds. If you are using pre-made pastry dough, then skip steps 2 and 3.

2.

Put the flour, cubed butter, and salt into a mixing bowl. Then, working quickly and gently, combine the butter into the flour with your fingertips or a pastry cutter, until the mixture resembles breadcrumbs.

3.

Add the cold water to the flour mixture 1 tablespoon at a time, and use your pastry cutter, or a cold knife, to mix the ingredients together. Stop stirring when the pastry comes together; do not overwork the dough. Wrap the dough in plastic and chill for 15–30 minutes.

4.

Unwrap the chilled dough that you made, or the chilled store-bought pastry dough, and place on a lightly floured surface. Using a rolling pin, roll out the dough to ¼ inch/½ cm thick. Using a tart mold or a cookie cutter, cut the pastry into circles that are slightly wider than your tart molds. Gently press the dough circles into each mold until the molds are filled to the top.

5.

Spoon your favorite jam into each tart until they are about three-quarters full. Do not overfill, or the jam will spill out and burn when it is baking. Bake for 15 minutes. Cool completely before you remove from the molds, then decorate or serve plain.

Aubrey and Avery are making miniature trifles on the day of the fair. They are using clear cups so everyone can see the layers.

MINI PINEAPPLE TRIFLES

Makes 6 servings

INGREDIENTS

1 cup/225g softened cream cheese
1 can pineapple tidbits
(or chunks cut into bite-sized pieces)
1 cup/60g whipped topping or
whipped cream
1 cup/100g crushed vanilla wafer cookies
additional fruit and whole cookies, to top

1.

Strain the juice from the canned pineapple and set aside. Crush some of the cookies until you have 1 cup of cookie crumbles. Don't crush them too much—you don't want cookie dust.

2.

In a medium bowl, beat the cream cheese until it is light and fluffy. Add 2 tablespoons of the pineapple juice and mix well. Stir in half the pineapple tidbits. Fold in the whipped topping or whipped cream until just mixed.

3.

In small serving dishes or cups, layer 1 tablespoon of the crushed cookies, then 1 or 2 tablespoons of the cream cheese mixture, and then 1 or 2 tablespoons of pineapple. Repeat these layers until the cup is filled. You will have 2 or 3 layers depending on the size of your cup. Top your mini trifles with more fruit and a whole cookie. The trifles should be eaten right away since the cookies can get soggy.

Zahira is using her grandfather's
shortbread cookie recipe.
He told her to always read the whole
recipe first before she starts baking.

NANKHATAI COOKIES

Makes 16–18 cookies

INGREDIENTS

1 cup/140g **flour**
½ cup/45g **gram flour**
2½ teaspoons **fine semolina**
½ cup/55g **powdered sugar**
pinch of **salt**
1 teaspoon **ground cardamom**
¾ cup/150g **ghee**
chopped pistachios for garnish

1.
Preheat the oven to 325 degrees Fahrenheit/ 160 degrees Celsius. Using a whisk, mix all of the dry ingredients together in a large bowl—the flour, gram flour, semolina, powered sugar, salt, and cardamom.

2.
Add the ghee to the dry mixture, and mix well with the dry ingredients using a spoon or your hands. The dough will be soft. If it feels sticky, sprinkle in a tiny bit more flour.

3.
Pinch the dough into 16–18 equal amounts, and roll them in your palms to make smooth balls. Slightly flatten the balls and place them on a parchment-lined cookie sheet with space between each ball, because they expand when baking. Using your thumb, press a slight indent into the middle of each ball, and press a few pistachios into each indent.

4.
Bake the cookies for 12–15 minutes, being careful not to let them get brown. The cookies should be very light in color. Cool completely before you handle them, because they crumble easily.

Hazel is helping her friend Lily bake apple custard muffins right after their team practice.

APPLE CUSTARD MUFFINS

1.

Grease the muffin tins and pre-heat the oven to 380 degrees Fahrenheit/195 degrees Celsius. In a bowl, whisk together the flour and the baking powder.

2.

In a large bowl, mix together the sugar, eggs, and salt until light and fluffy. Stir in the vanilla and the milk, then add in the cooled, melted butter and mix well to make a batter. Add the flour mixture to the batter, and mix all the ingredients together.

3.

Peel and core the apples and chop into small chunks. Ask a grown-up for help when using a knife. Gently add the apples to the batter, making sure that they are well coated.

4.

Spoon the batter into the prepared muffin tins. The batter will be lumpy. Bake for 18 minutes or until the muffin tops are golden-brown and a toothpick inserted into the center comes out clean. Dust the tops with powdered sugar if you like.

Makes 10 standard-sized muffins

INGREDIENTS

3 medium apples—Gala, Fuji, or Granny Smith (for a tart flavor) work well
½ cup/70g flour
1 teaspoon baking powder
⅓ cup/65g sugar
2 large eggs
pinch of salt
2 teaspoons vanilla extract
6 tablespoons/90ml milk
2 tablespoons/30g butter, melted
powdered sugar for dusting (optional)

Sakura is spending the afternoon making mochi for the fair. She picked the strawberries from the garden herself.

STRAWBERRY MOCHI

1.

Wash, dry, and hull the strawberries. Divide the bean paste into 6 equal balls. Flatten each ball into a round disc and wrap each strawberry completely in the paste. The paste is very sticky, so you will need to wash and dry your hands often. If your hands are clean each time you start working with a strawberry, it will be easier to work with the paste.

2.

In a microwavable glass bowl, mix the sweet rice flour and the sugar together. Slowly add the water, stirring constantly until the dough mixture is thick and smooth.

3.

Cover the bowl with plastic wrap and microwave for 1 minute. Be very careful when you lift the plastic wrap—it will be hot! Stir the mixture. Cover with plastic wrap again and microwave for 1 more minute, then, using caution, stir again. Repeat one last time for 30 seconds. The dough mixture should start to look a little translucent. It is best to do this in 3 steps because the mixture needs to be stirred each time.

4.

Sprinkle the cornstarch on a tray and spoon out the mochi dough onto the starch. Turn over the mochi dough in the starch. The starch will make it less sticky to work with. Divide the mochi dough into 6 equal pieces and flatten each into a 3 inch/8 cm round disk.

5.

Working on 1 strawberry at a time, place a paste-covered strawberry in the middle of a mochi disk, and form the dough around each strawberry so that it makes a ball. Pinch the dough closed at the bottom and twist. The mochi should be eaten within 2 days.

Mochi are very chewy and sticky, so it is best to take small bites and chew carefully.

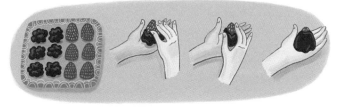

Makes 6 mochi. If you want to make more mochi, repeat this recipe as many times as you like, because it is best to work in small batches.

INGREDIENTS

6 **medium-sized whole strawberries**
½ cup/150g **store-bought red bean paste**
¾ cup/100g **sweet rice flour**
1½ tablespoons **sugar**
½ cup plus 2 tablespoons/150ml **water**
cornstarch for dusting
(approximately ¼ cup/50g)

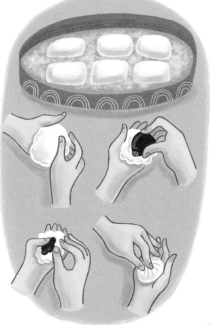

Layla has never made a basbousa cake, but she has watched her mother make it many times. Now she feels ready to make one on her own.

BASBOUSA CAKE

1.

Preheat the oven to 350 degrees Fahrenheit/180 degrees Celsius. To prepare your pan, add a round piece of 9 inch/23 cm parchment to the bottom, and grease the parchment and the sides of the pan. In a large bowl, combine all the dry ingredients—the flours, coconut, sugar, salt, and baking powder—and mix well. Add the yogurt, eggs, and vanilla and stir until well blended.

2.

Bake the cake for 20–25 minutes until a knife inserted into the center comes out clean. While the cake is baking, make the sugar syrup. With the help of a grown-up, in a saucepan, combine the sugar and water and simmer over high heat until the sugar is dissolved. Keep simmering for around 10 minutes to make a light syrup. Add the lemon juice and allow the syrup to cool slightly.

3.

After you take your cake out of the oven, while it is still in the pan, slowly pour the syrup over the warm cake to coat the whole cake. When the cake is completely cool, carefully take it out of the pan and decorate with the nuts and coconut. This cake is best served the next day.

Makes one 9 inch/23 cm round cake

CAKE INGREDIENTS

2 cups/330g fine semolina flour
2 cups/280g flour
2 cups/160g unsweetened coconut flakes
2 cups/400g sugar
1 teaspoon salt
2 teaspoons baking powder
1 cup/250g plain whole-milk yogurt
3 large eggs
2 teaspoons vanilla extract

SYRUP INGREDIENTS

1¼ cups/250g granulated sugar
1¼ cups/300ml water
1 teaspoon lemon juice

TOPPING

chopped pistachios and unsweetened coconut flakes to taste

Jamie has been experimenting with gluten-free recipes and will bring a family favorite cake to the fair.

GLUTEN-FREE CARROT CAKE

1.

Preheat the oven to 350 degrees Fahrenheit/ 180 degrees Celsius and grease and line the loaf pan with parchment.

2.

In a large bowl, whisk together the eggs, sugar, maple syrup, oil, and vanilla until blended. Add in the flours, baking powder, spices, and salt, then stir until fully combined.

3.

Peel and grate the carrots, then gently fold into the batter. Stir in any optional add-ins. Pour the batter into the prepared loaf pan.

4.

Bake for 40—45 minutes until a toothpick inserted into the center comes out clean. Let the cake cool before taking it out of the pan. To make the optional glaze: whisk all ingredients together. If the glaze is too thick you can add a tiny bit more almond milk, starting with around 1 teaspoon, until it has reached the desired consistency. Spread the glaze over the cake.

Makes one 8x5 inch/20x13 cm loaf cake

CAKE INGREDIENTS

4 large eggs
½ cup/100g sugar
2 tablespoons maple syrup
⅓ cup/80ml melted coconut oil
1½ teaspoons vanilla extract
1⅔ cups/160g almond flour
¼ cup/30g coconut flour
1½ teaspoons gluten-free baking powder
1 teaspoon ground cinnamon
¼ teaspoon nutmeg
⅛ teaspoon ground cloves
⅛ teaspoon salt
1 cup/110g grated carrots (from about 2 medium carrots)
½ cup/100g raisins
½ cup/65g chopped walnuts (optional)

GLAZE INGREDIENTS (optional)

½ cup/55g powdered sugar
1 tablespoon maple syrup
1—2 tablespoons almond milk

Hazel could not have imagined a better bake sale for the school library, and she is so proud of her friends!

BAKE SALE for the Library

BEFORE YOU BEGIN BAKING

Always wash your hands and make sure your work surface is clean.

Read the whole recipe before you start, and ask a grown-up if you have any questions. Take your time; there is no need to rush.

Gather all of the ingredients, bowls, and tools you will need to make sure that you have everything before you start.

Preheat your oven and prepare your baking pans or trays as needed.

Baking requires exact measurements, so measure carefully. When measuring dry ingredients, be sure to level the ingredients and not overfill your measuring cups or spoons. For liquids, fill up to the precise line on the measuring cup you are using.

Do not skip any steps or ingredients. Baking is a science and if an ingredient or a step is missed, the baked item won't turn out well.

Be very careful when using a knife, peeler, grater, or mixer. Ask a grown-up for help when using these tools.

Be very careful when using the oven, stove, or microwave. Always use oven mitts or potholders. Ask a grown-up for help when using these appliances.

Remember to ask a grown-up for advice if you are unsure whether your baked item has finished cooking.

Follow the recipe instructions for cooling your baked item before removing it from the pan or tray.

After you are finished, clean up and put all unused ingredients away.

HAVE FUN AND WHEN YOU ARE ALL DONE, PLEASE SHARE WHAT YOU MADE WITH OTHERS!

© 2021, Prestel Verlag, Munich · London · New York
A member of Penguin Random House Verlagsgruppe GmbH
Neumarkter Strasse 28 · 81673 Munich
© text & illustrations: 2021, Cynthia Cliff

Library of Congress Control Number: 2020948550
A CIP catalogue record for this book is available from the British Library.

Editorial direction: Doris Kutschbach
Copyediting: Martha Jay
Design, layout, production management: Susanne Hermann
Separations: Reproline Mediateam
Printing and binding: DZS Grafik

Prestel Publishing compensates the CO$_2$ emissions produced from the making
of this book by supporting a reforestation project in Brazil. Find further
information on the project here: www.ClimatePartner.com/14044-1912-1001

Penguin Random House Verlagsgruppe FSC® N001967
Printed in Slovenia
ISBN 978-3-7913-7460-4

www.prestel.com